sun

mercury

venus

earth

moon

mars

jupiter

saturn

uranus

neptune

GOODNIGHT EVERYONE

No dreamer is ever too small, no dream is ever too big.
— anonymous

For my sister, Jan, a Montessori teacher,
who inspired the idea of this book.

First U.S. edition 2016

Library of Congress Catalog Card Number pending
ISBN 978-0-7636-9079-3

16 17 18 19 20 21 APS 10 9 8 7 6 5 4 3 2 1

Printed in Humen, Dongguan, China

This book was typeset in SHH.
The illustrations were created digitally.

Candlewick Press
99 Dover Street
Somerville, Massachusetts 02144

visit us at www.candlewick.com

CANDLEWICK PRESS

the sun is going down and everyone is sleepy

the mice

are sleepy

...YAWN

"aren't you tired?" ask the deer

"oh no, no! not even a little bit,"

says Little Bear

but after a
while, Little
Bear sighs

AH....................

takes a
long, deep
breath

AHHHH............................

and has a

GREAT, BIG,

ENORMOUS

s t r e t c h

AHHHH.........

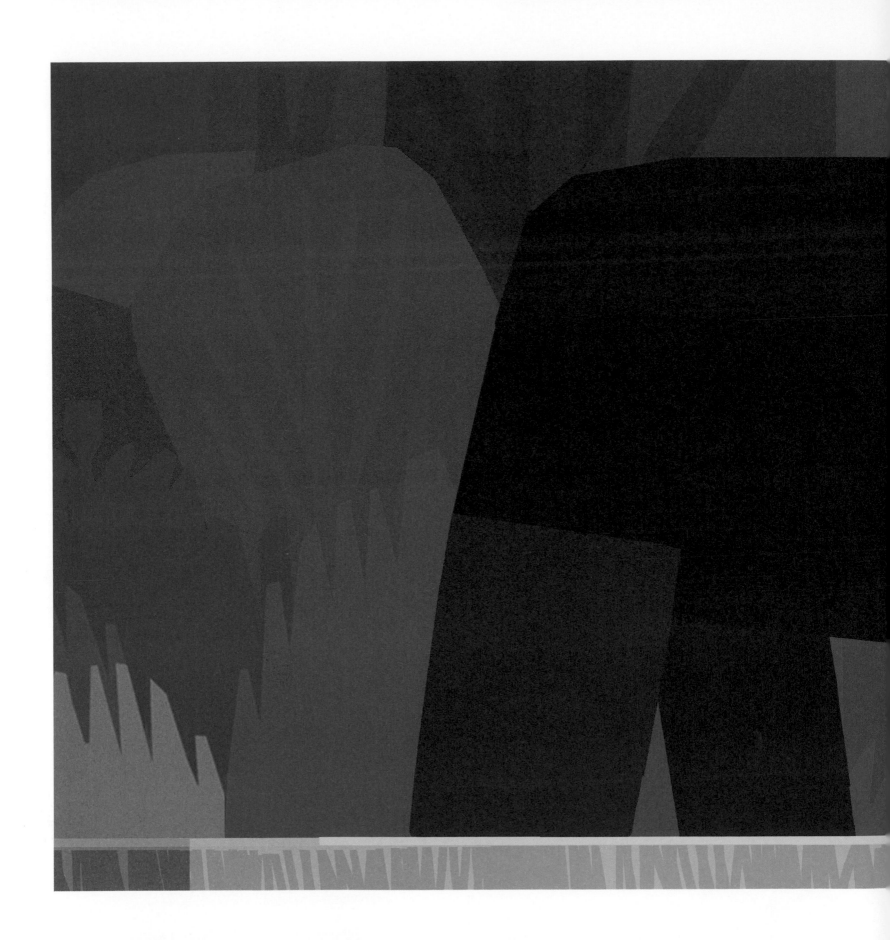

"it really must
be time for bed,"
says Great
Big Bear

the mice are asleep

they snore

. . . z Z Z

and sigh

S S s . . .

goodnight mice

the hares are asleep

...zzzZZZ

SSSSss...

goodnight hares

the deer are asleep

...zzzZZZZZ

SSSSSSss...

goodnight deer

Little Bear
gets a great
big goodnight
kiss

:X:

goodnight bears

goodnight everyone

the moon is high and everyone is fast asleep

neptune

uranus

saturn

jupiter

mars

moon

earth

venus

mercury

sun